The Hedgehog
Who Wanted to Be
a Squirrel

The Hedgehog Who Wanted to Be a Squirrel

David Webster

Illustrated by Emily Webster

The Hedgehog Who Wanted to be a Squirrel
David Webster

Published by Aspect Design 2020
Malvern, Worcestershire, United Kingdom.

Designed, printed and bound by Aspect Design
89 Newtown Road, Malvern, Worcs. WR14 1PD
United Kingdom
Tel: 01684 561567
E-mail: allan@aspect-design.net
Website: www.aspect-design.net

Cover Design Copyright © 2020 Aspect Design
Cover art Copyright © 2020 Emily Webster
ISBN 978-1-912078-19-6

Henry the hedgehog was feeling sad.

Peeping out of his cosy home under the log pile, he was watching Sam the squirrel. How he longed to be like Sam!

Sam could leap around in the trees, jumping nimbly from branch to branch. Sam had lovely smooth fur, and a great bushy tail which he flicked and waved. Sam had shiny whiskers and bright eyes.

Henry had none of these. He had sharp prickles, and could only shuffle along the ground. How he longed to be like Sam! He wanted so much to be a squirrel.

Then one day Henry made up his mind. He would change! He would become a squirrel!

But first he must learn to climb trees.

He crept out of his little home, and went in search of a tree. He needed one that was easy to climb; one to learn on. Soon he found an ideal tree. Its trunk leaned, so it was not too steep to climb.

He took hold of the bark with his little paws, and began to heave himself up.

'Heave! Heave!' he thought, panting for breath.

'Little by little! Careful!'

How he wished that he had sharp claws like Sam! Soon his little feet got tired . . . and he began to slip.

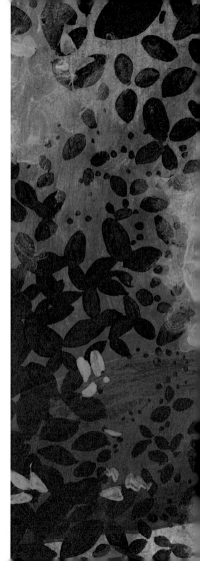

'Whoah!' he cried.
And
     he
          fell
               from
                    the
                         tree.
He just had
time to curl up into
a ball before he hit
the ground.

Crump!

He bounced.

Once.

Twice.

Boing!

Boing!

Then he came to rest.

He slowly uncurled himself, and looked sadly at one or two bent prickles.

'Oh dear!' he said to himself.

'Oh dear!

'Oh dear!'

Next day, when he peeped out and saw Sam leaping around on a branch of the conker tree, Henry decided to try again to change.

Perhaps if he looked more like a squirrel then he would be able to behave more like a squirrel.

It was his prickles that were the problem. Sam didn't have prickles. Sam had fur.

Henry decided that the first thing he needed to do was to get rid of his prickles.

Then he would buy a fur coat. Surely that would work!

So Henry went along to Willy Woodpecker the Hairdresser.

'Please,' he said, 'will you pull out my prickles?'

'Pull out your prickles!' said Willy Woodpecker, very shocked. 'Why?'

'I want to be a squirrel,' said Henry. 'So please do as I ask.'

'Well that sounds very odd to me. Let's start with just a few,' said Willy.

Oh dear! It wasn't at all easy.

No matter how hard Willy pulled, the prickles would not budge.

He even called his wife, Wilhelmina, to help him, but with both of them pulling the prickles still wouldn't budge.

'That hurts!' said Henry.

'It's no use trying any more,' said Willy.

So Henry went back to his little house, very sad.

Next day Henry watched Sam busy digging holes in the soft earth, looking for buried acorns. He had a good think. He couldn't climb trees like Sam. He couldn't have soft fur like Sam.

But perhaps if he ate the same kind of food as Sam he would change into a squirrel. Perhaps if he ate acorns and conkers and nuts, instead of worms and beetles . . . Perhaps!

When Sam had gone back up the tree Henry shuffled and snuffled out of his house, and began to dig for acorns.

Suddenly he came across a long, fat, wiggly worm.

'Ooooh! What a treat!' he thought.

But then he remembered – it was to be acorns, not worms.

'No more worms!' he said firmly to himself.

So Henry kept digging.

Then he noticed, lying on the ground, an acorn that Sam had missed. He scurried over, and began to nibble it. It was so hard! And it tasted so bitter!

The acorn wasn't all soft and squidgy like a lovely worm. His teeth weren't like Sam's. They weren't made for chewing hard nuts.

Soon he gave up, and crept home, hungry, and wishing he had eaten that delicious worm after all.

That night Henry felt very sad. What could he do? He so wanted to be a squirrel, but nothing was working. Then he had a bright idea. He would go and see the Wise Owl. He would know what to do.

He found Wise Owl sitting on the branch of a tree – the same branch that Sam had been running up and down.

'Please, Mr Wise Owl,' he said, 'Can you help me? I want to be a squirrel.'

Mr Wise Owl blinked once. Then twice. He cocked his head on one side, and looked down at Henry with his wide eyes.

'I beg your pardon,' he said. 'Did you say that you want to be a squirrel?'

'Yes!' said Henry excitedly. 'I want to run and jump and climb trees and flick a long bushy tail and be soft and fluffy and eat nuts.'

Mr Wise Owl shut his eyes, and became very quiet for a while. Henry thought he might have gone to sleep, but he was thinking.

At last Wise Owl opened one eye. Then the other.

He said, 'Hmmmm!'

He cocked his head on one side, and then on the other.

And then he said slowly, 'Now listen to me, Henry! You are a hedgehog. You are not a squirrel. Your mother and father are hedgehogs. They are not squirrels.

'Now Sam's mother and father are squirrels. So Sam is a squirrel.

'But you can never be a squirrel. You are what you are – **a lovely, clever hedgehog.**

'You have beautiful, shiny prickles, that protect you.

'You can roll up into a ball.

'You have a very handsome face, with a lovely, turned-up nose and soft eyes.

'You can go about at night, in the dark, when squirrels are all in bed.

'You don't dig holes all over people's lawns, burying your food and then forgetting where you buried it. You are too clever to do that. And you get rid of nasty slugs by eating them. You should be very proud to be a hedgehog. Very content to be who you are.

'Remember, you are you. **You are special!**

'I guess,' said Mr Wise Owl, before closing his eyes to make it clear that his speech was finished, 'I guess that Sam the squirrel often looks at you, **and wishes that he was a hedgehog!'**

Henry could see that Wise Owl had finished what he had to say. He waited a bit in case he might open his eyes and speak again, but he didn't. And so Henry shuffled and snuffled back to his cosy home under the log pile.

As he shuffled along he thought how lovely the soft, damp earth felt under his little feet. How much better than the hard, rough tree bark. And he thought how rich the soil smelt.

He ate a particularly delicious beetle that he came across, and he thought how much better it tasted than that acorn.

And when he reached his cosy home he thought how much better it was than a home of sticks, high in a windy tree.

He looked in his mirror, and he thought, 'Yes! Yes! I do like the way I look. I do like my little turned-up nose, and my dark eyes, and my smart, shiny prickles.

'Yes!' he thought to himself. 'Yes! Mr Wise Owl is right! I am who I am! I am lucky to be who I am!

'I am a hedgehog. I am glad that I am a hedgehog. In fact I am proud to be a hedgehog.

'I am content!'

And with that, he curled up into a ball, gave a happy sigh, and went to sleep.